Ballet
COLORING
BOOK!

Discover This Collection Of Coloring Pages For Girls

Bold Illustrations
COLORING BOOKS

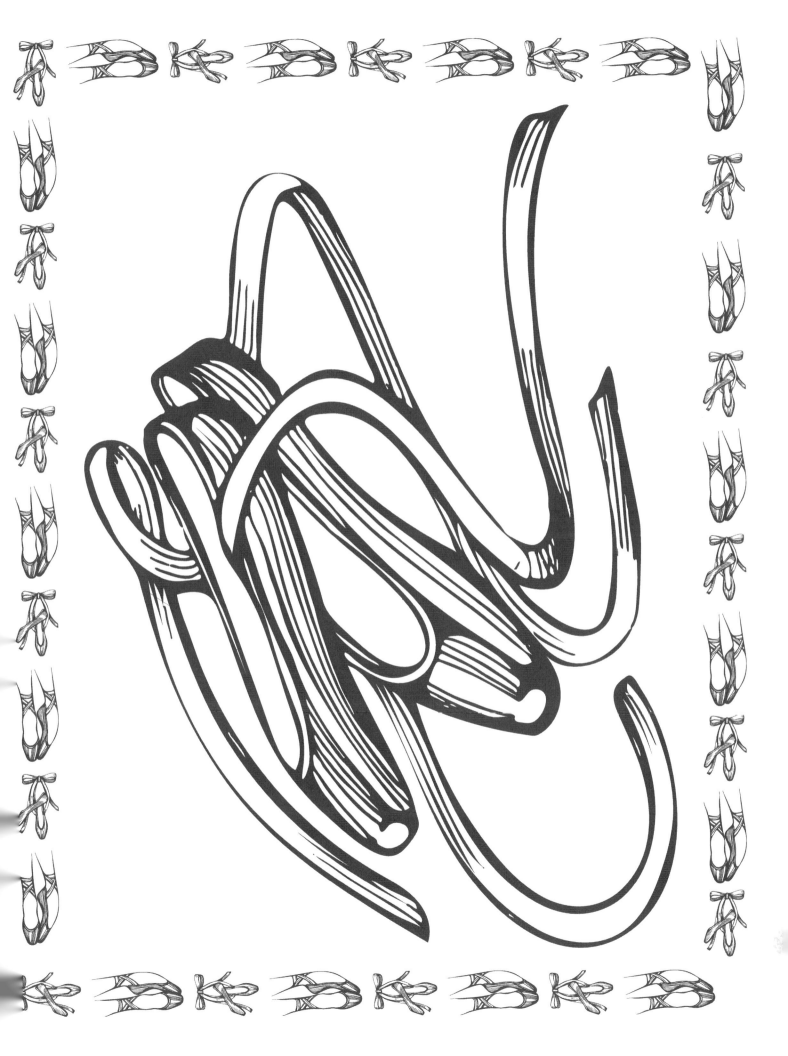

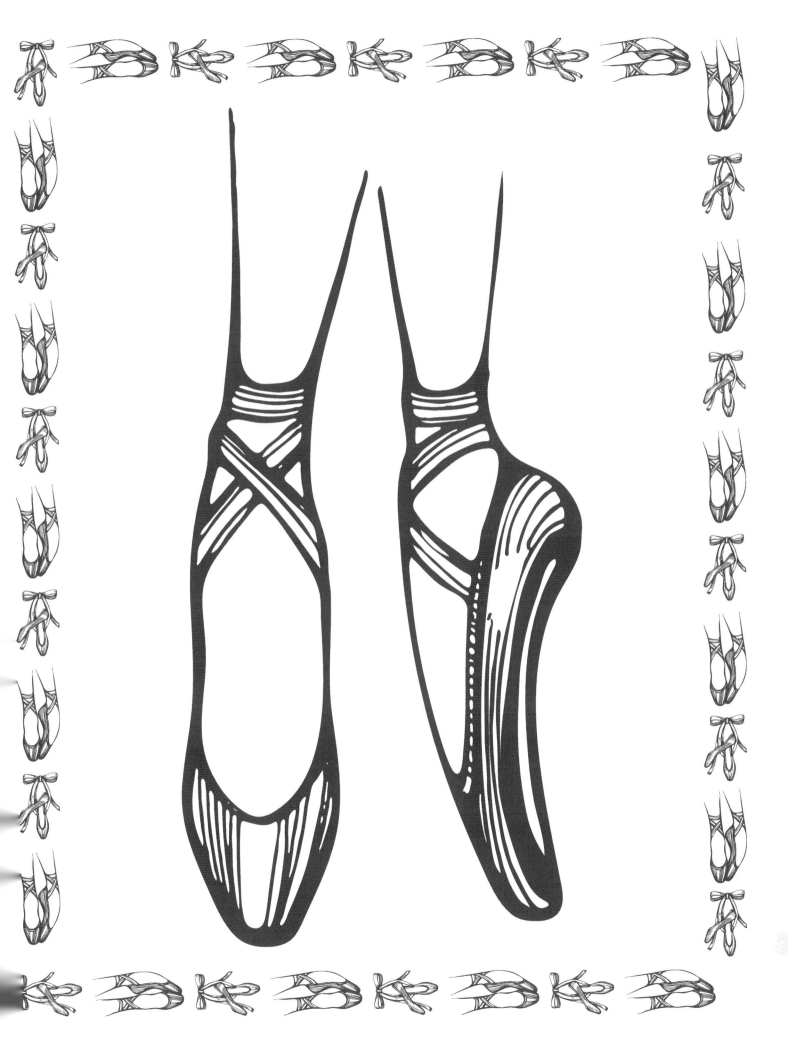

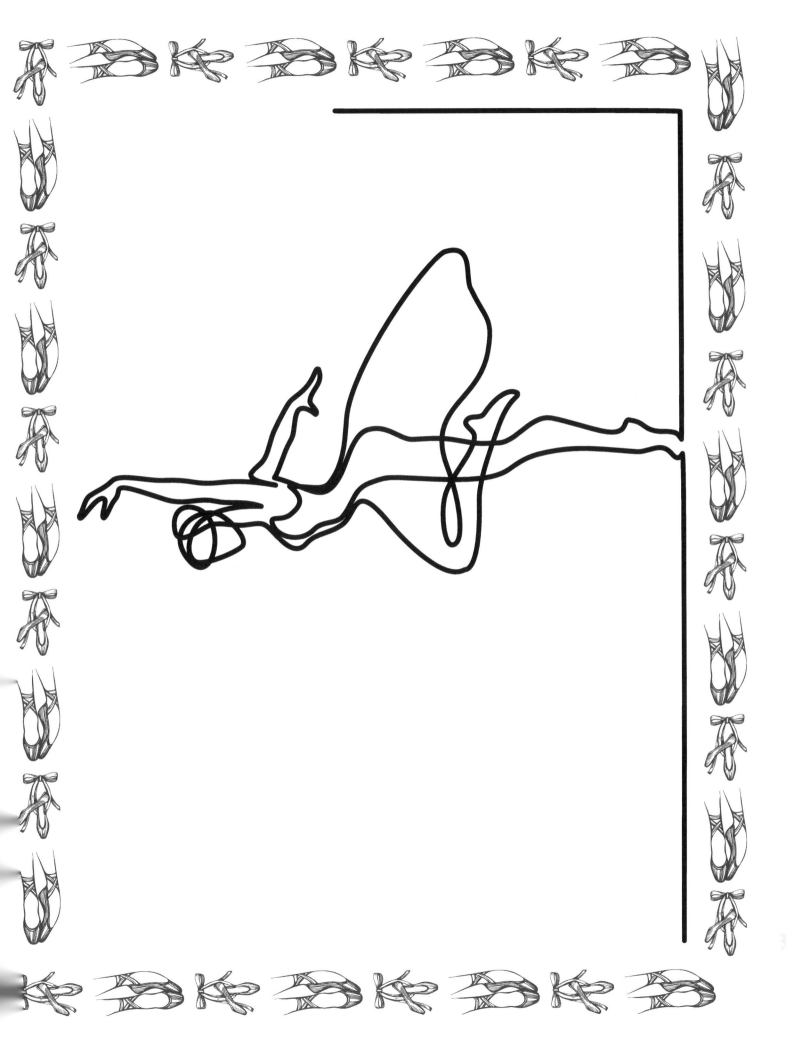

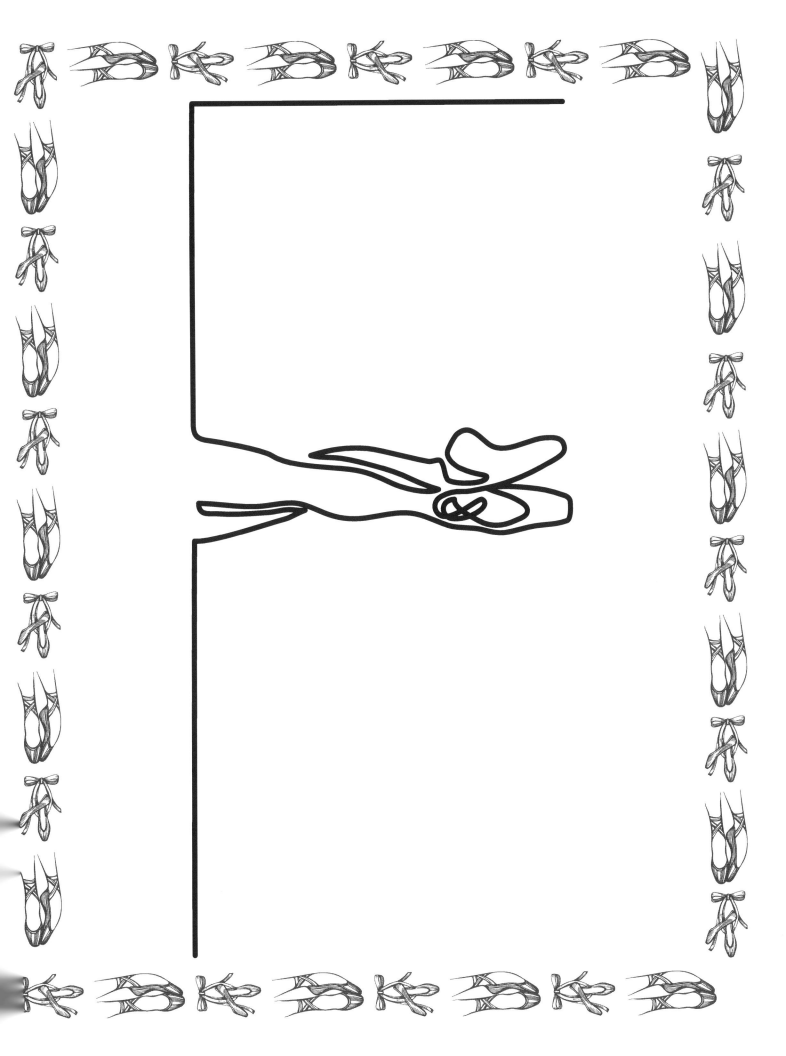

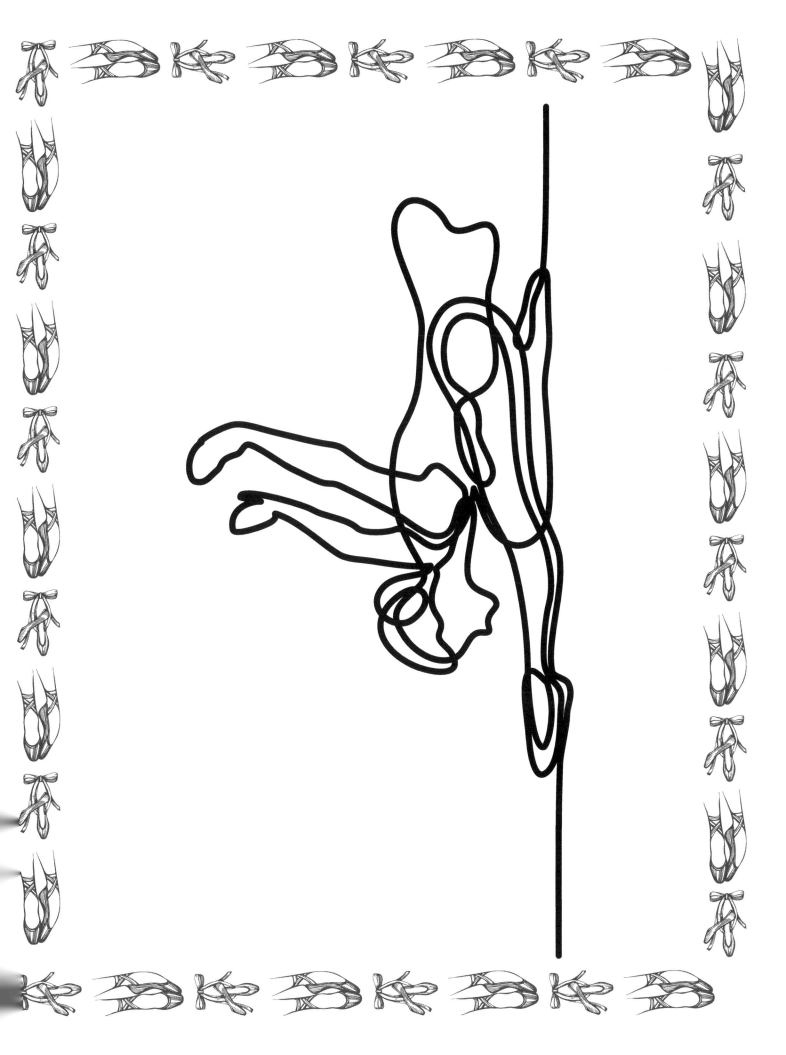

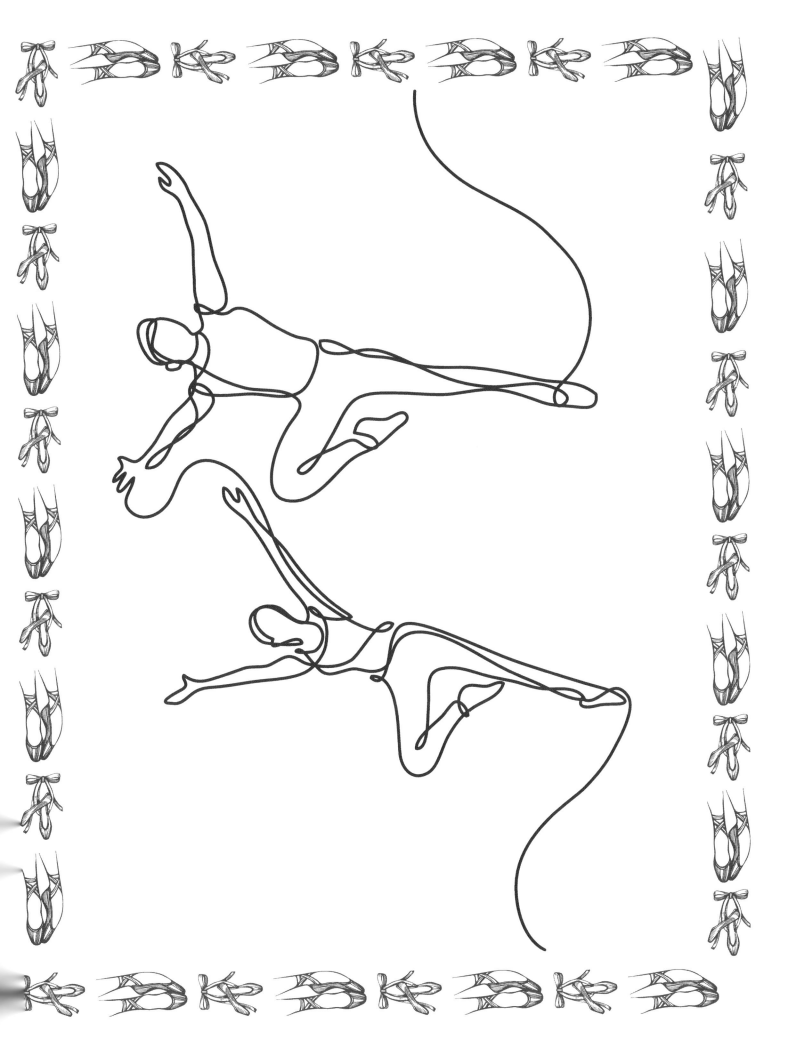

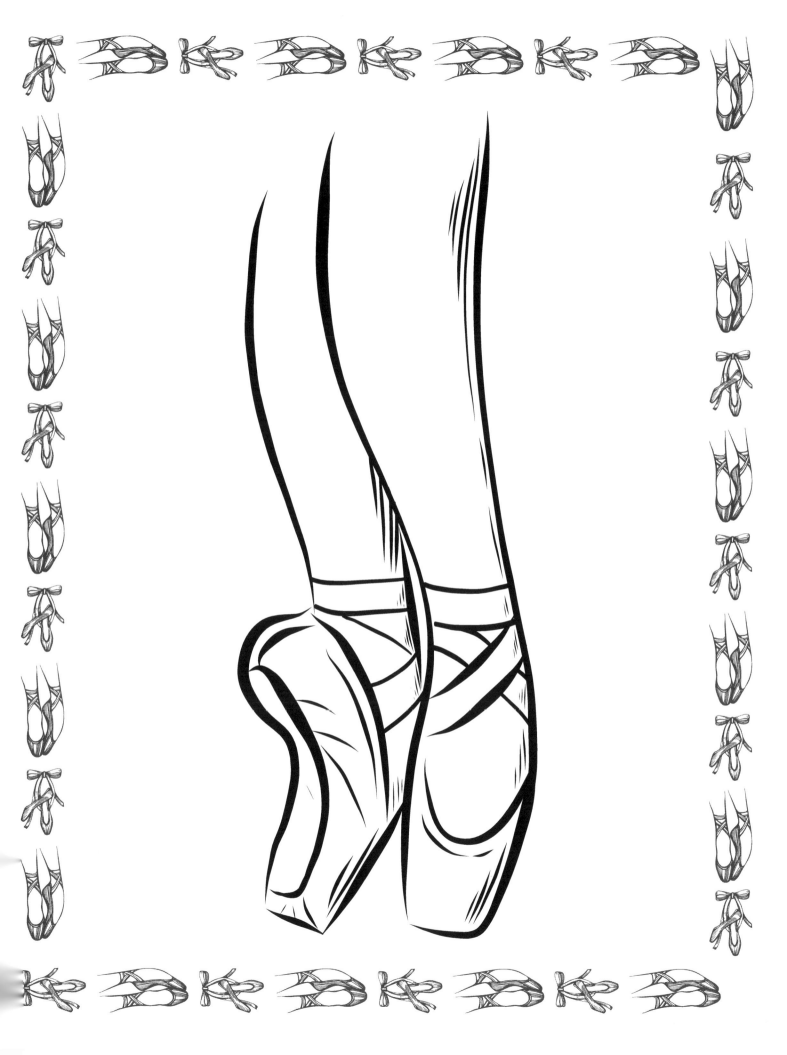

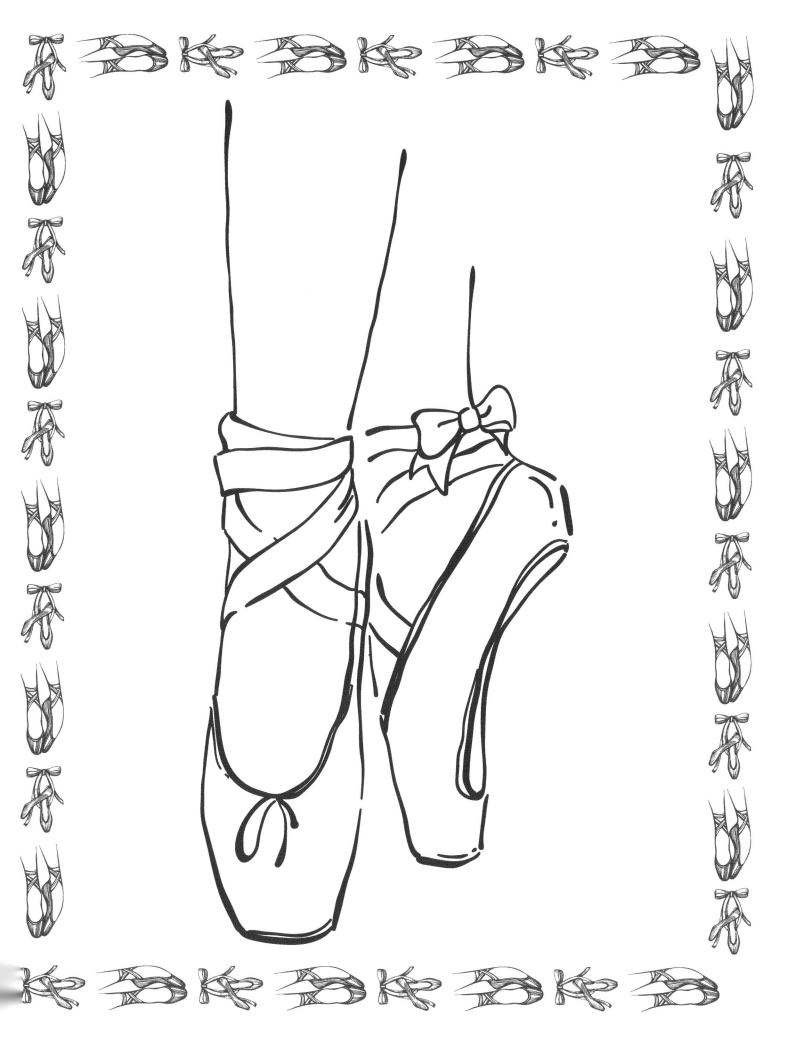

This is a Bleed Through Page If You Are Using a Colouring Marker or Pen!
Find Other Great Titles By searching for <u>Bold Illustrations</u> on Your Favorite Book Retailer
Amazon.Ca | Barnes & Noble (BN.Com) | Books A Million (BAM.Com)

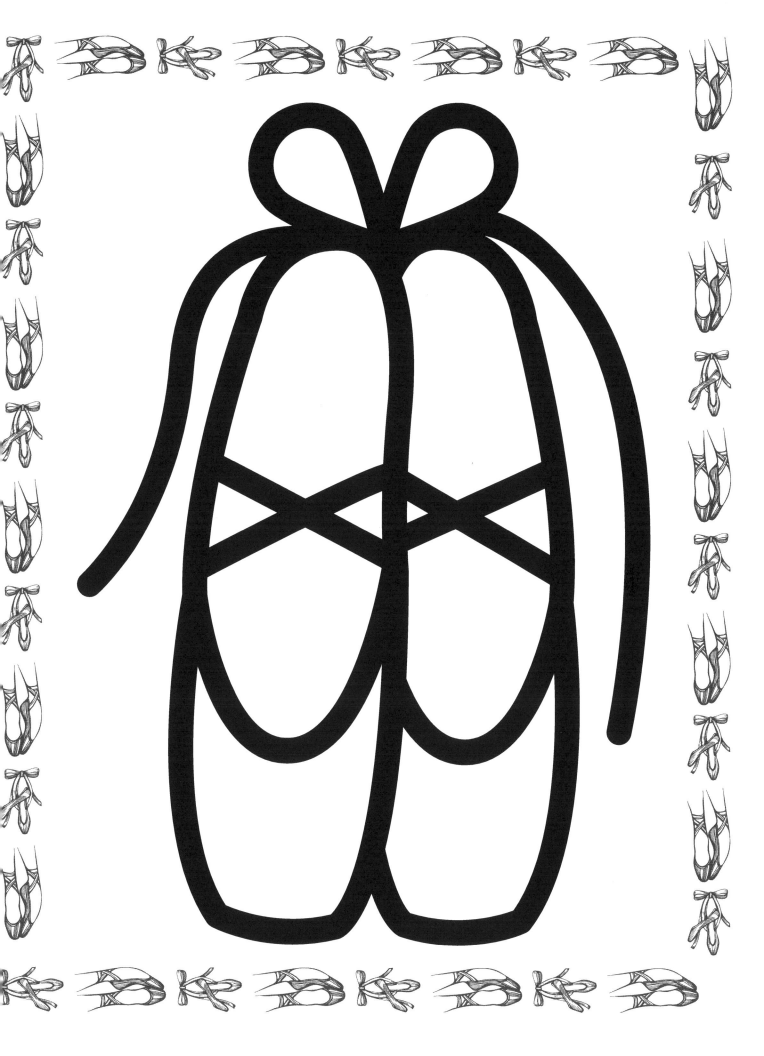

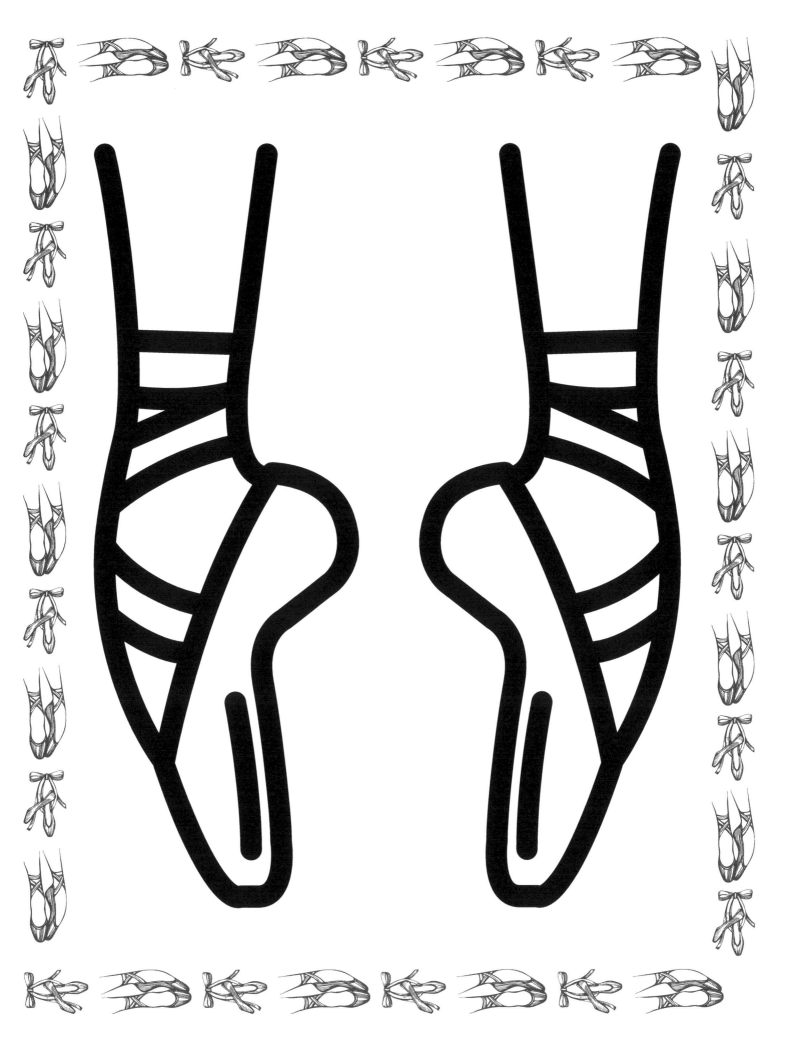

This is a Bleed Through Page If You Are Using a Colouring Marker or Pen!
Find Other Great Titles By searching for <u>Bold Illustrations</u> on Your Favorite Book Retailer
Amazon.Ca | Barnes & Noble (BN.Com) | Books A Million (BAM.Com)

This is a Bleed Through Page If You Are Using a Colouring Marker or Pen!
Find Other Great Titles By searching for <u>*Bold Illustrations*</u> *on Your Favorite Book Retailer*
Amazon.Ca | Barnes & Noble (BN.Com) | Books A Million (BAM.Com)

Made in the USA
Middletown, DE
16 July 2020